The Butterfly House

By Ben Walker

Illustrated by Richard Hoit

Jake and Emma and Dad
went to the zoo.

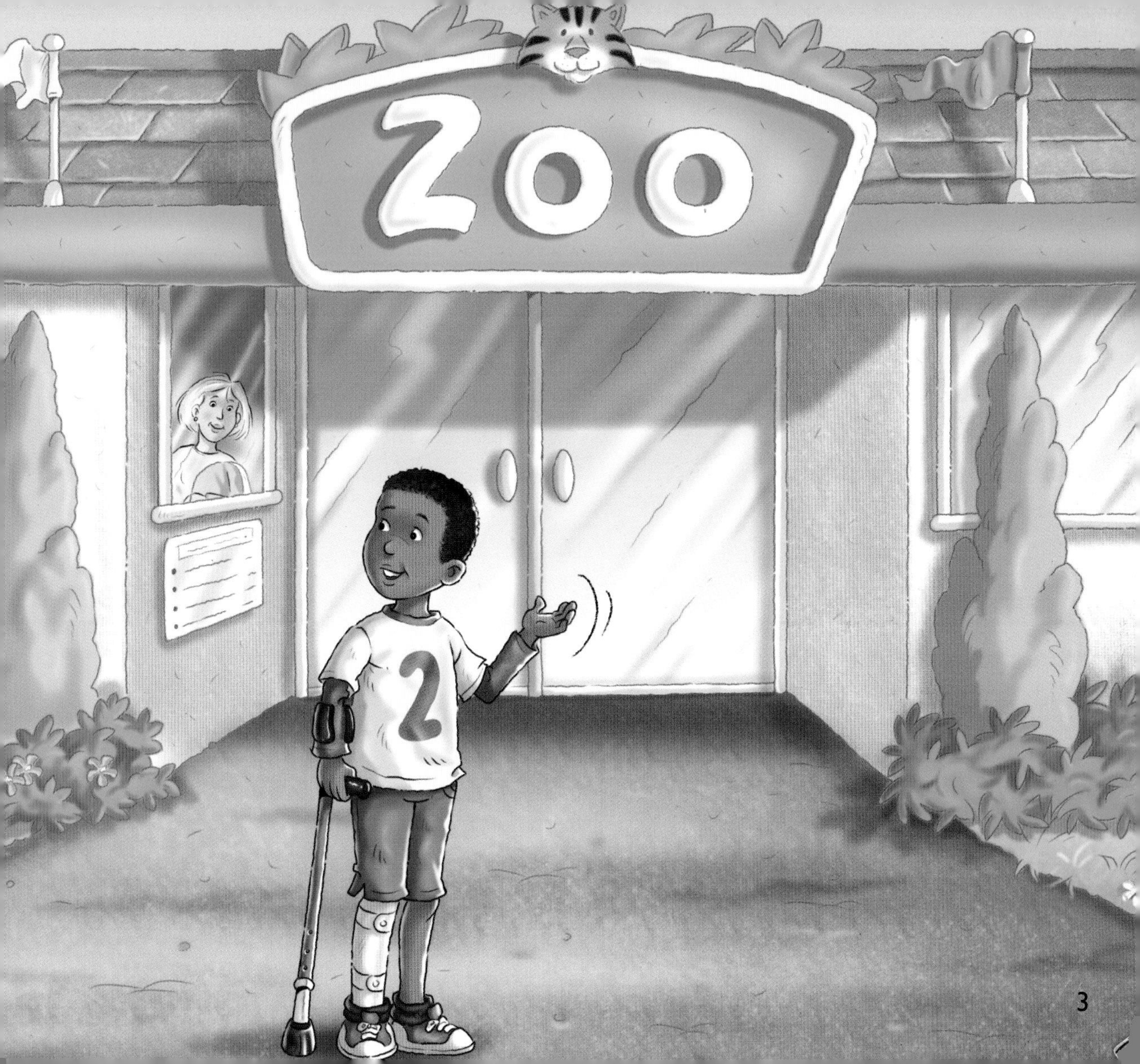
ZOO
2

"I like butterflies," said Emma.
"Can we go and see
the butterflies?"

Butterfly House

Birds

Tigers

Bears

"I do not like butterflies," said Jake.
"I am not going in the butterfly house."

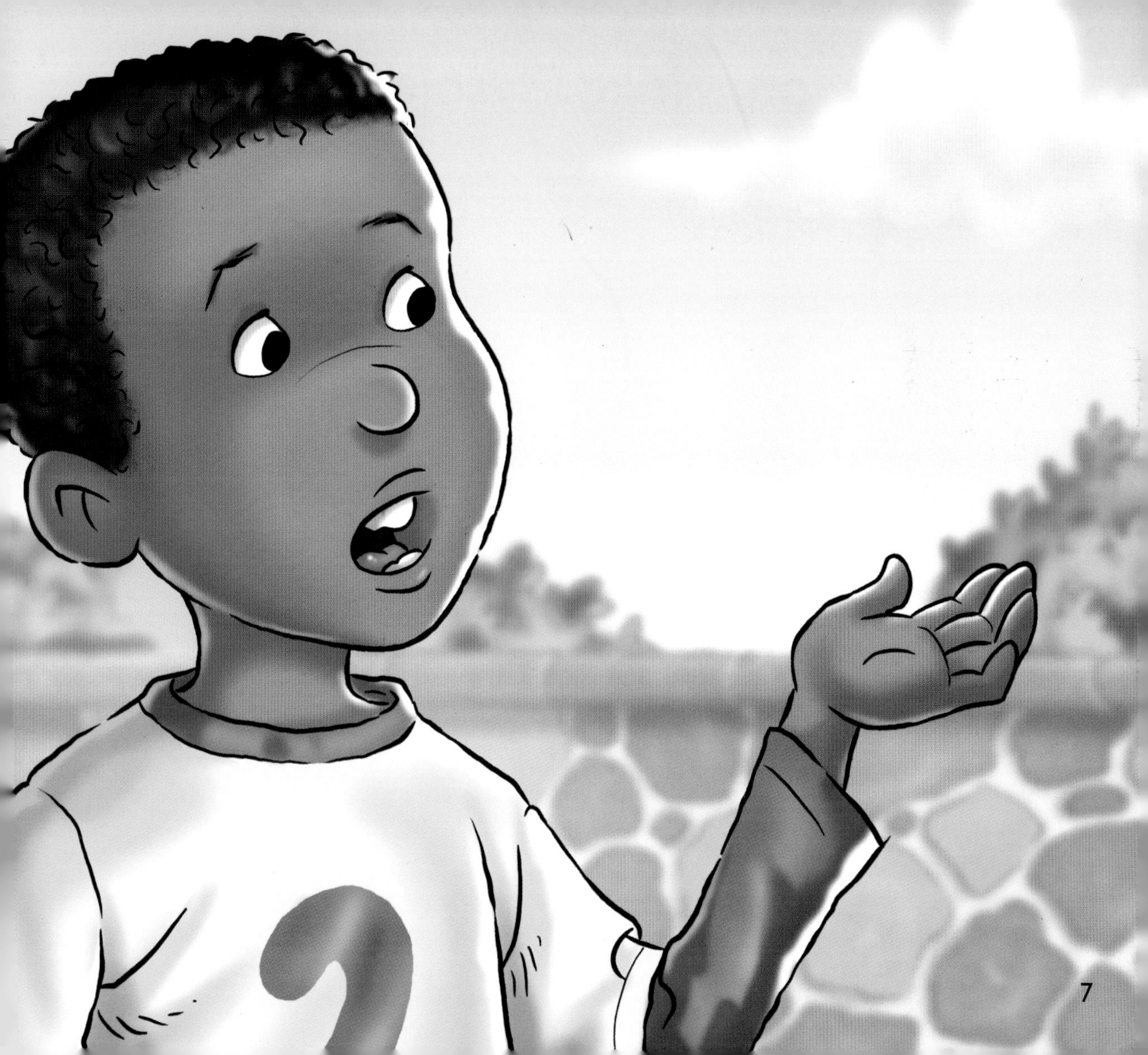

"Come on, Jake," said Dad.

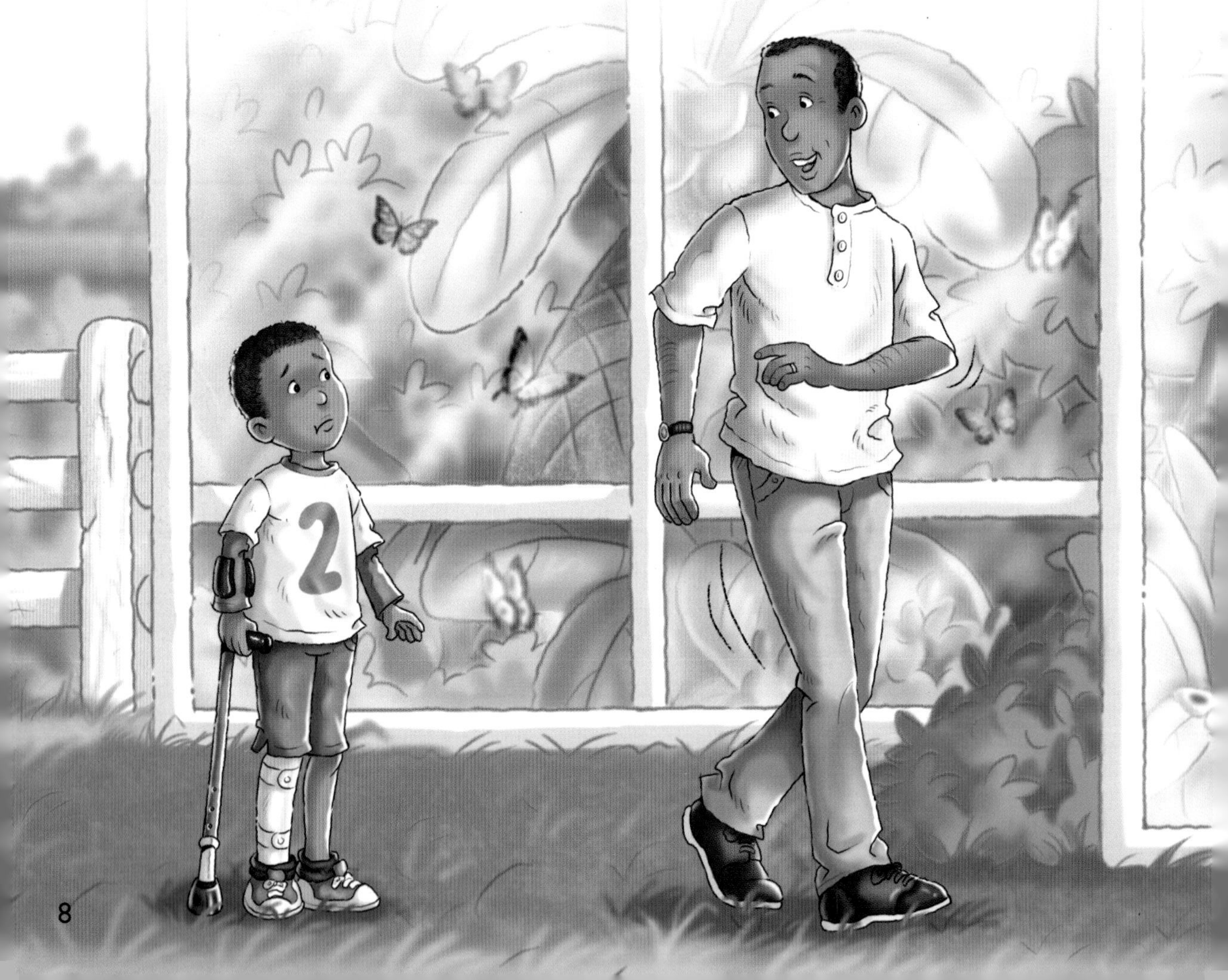
2

Emma and Jake and Dad
went into the butterfly house.

"Look!" said Emma.
"Look at the
big blue butterflies!"

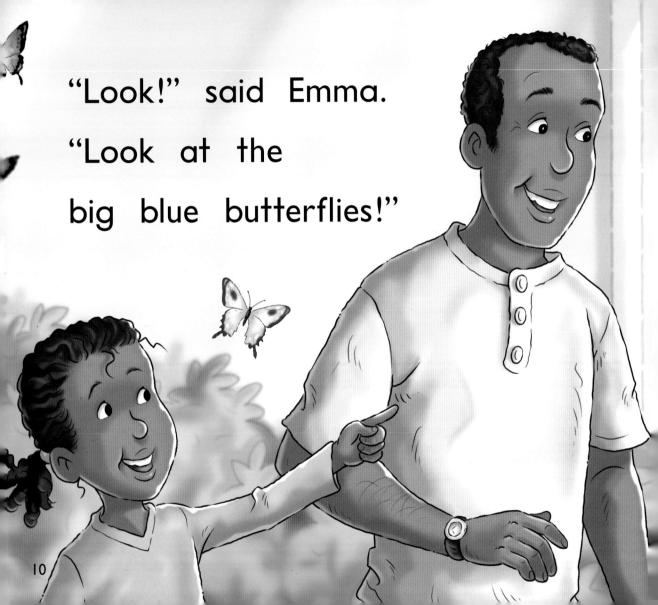

Jake looked up.

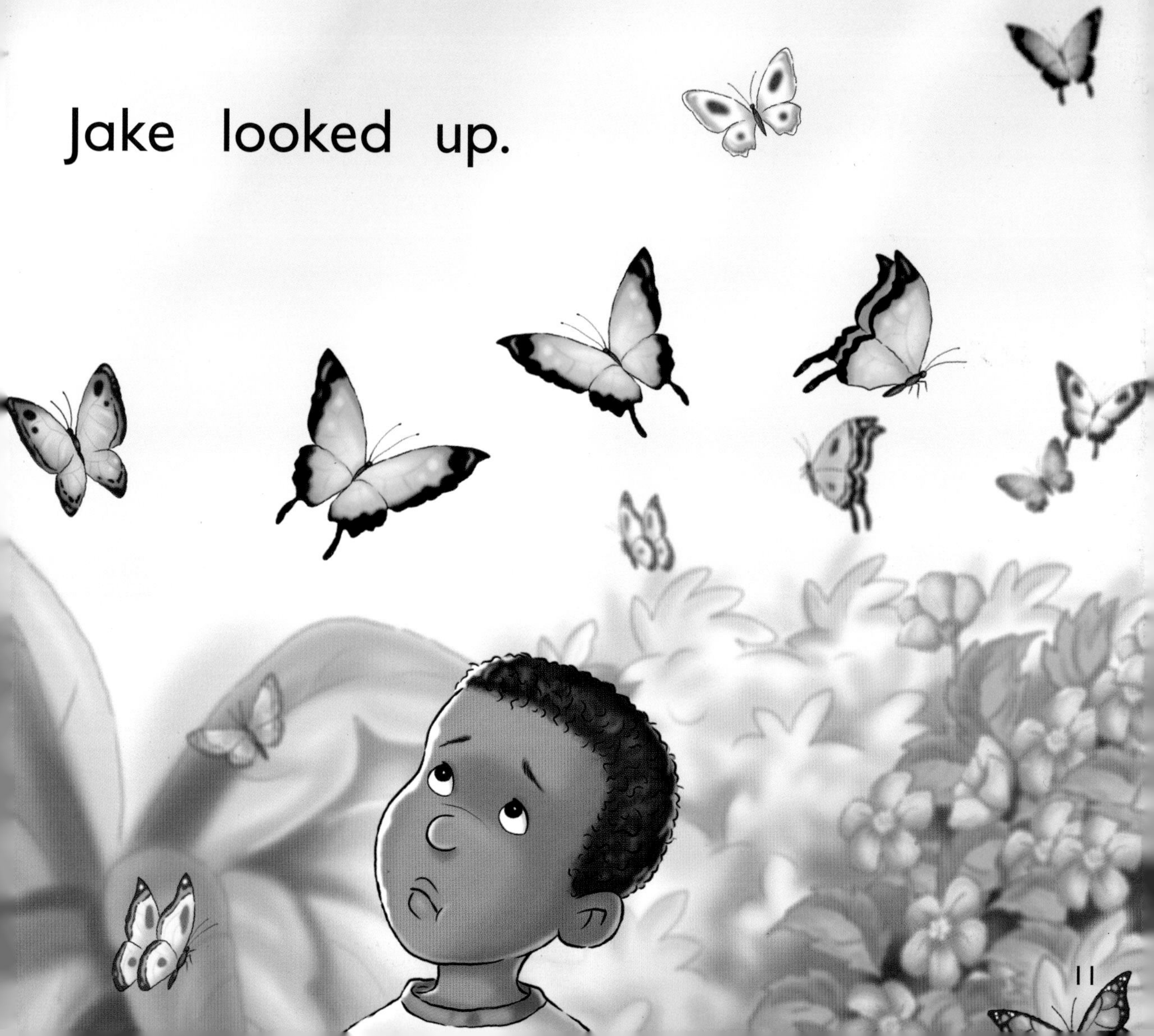

"Oh!" said Jake.

"A butterfly is on me!"

12

"Look, Dad!" said Emma.

"A blue butterfly is on Jake."

"A butterfly is on Emma, too!"
said Jake.

"Yes," said Emma. "Look!

Look at me.

Look at the butterflies!"

"I do like the butterfly house," said Jake.

"I do like butterflies, too!"